Based on the real-life story of
Helen Keller and Martha Washington

Hand in Hand

Jean Little

Illustrated by
Norman Lanting

Scholastic Canada Ltd.
Toronto New York London Auckland Sydney
Mexico City New Delhi Hong Kong Buenos Aires

Scholastic Canada Ltd.
604 King Street West, Toronto, Ontario M5V 1E1, Canada

Scholastic Inc.
557 Broadway, New York, NY 10012, USA

Scholastic Australia Pty Limited
PO Box 579, Gosford, NSW 2250, Australia

Scholastic New Zealand Limited
Private Bag 94407, Botany, Manukau 2163, New Zealand

Scholastic Children's Books
Euston House, 24 Eversholt Street, London NW1 1DB, UK

www.scholastic.ca

Library and Archives Canada Cataloguing in Publication
Little, Jean, 1932-, author
Hand in hand / by Jean Little ; illustrations by Norman
Lanting.
Issued in print and electronic formats.
ISBN 978-1-4431-3923-6 (paperback).--ISBN 978-1-4431-4693-7
(html)
1. Keller, Helen, 1880-1968--Juvenile fiction. I. Lanting,
Norm, illustrator II. Title.

PS8523.I77H36 2016   jC813'.54   C2016-902187-4
                                               C2016-902188-2

Photo credits: Cover photo, hands by Kathryn Hollinrake Photography,
© 2016 by Scholastic Canada Ltd.
Cover photo, daisy field © Alekss/Fotolia.
Illustrations copyright © 2016 by Scholastic Canada Ltd.

6 5 4 3 2 1   Printed in Canada 121   16 17 18 19 20

"In those days, Martha Washington, the child of our cook, and Belle, an old setter who had been a great hunter in her day, were my constant companions. Martha Washington understood my signs and I seldom had any difficulty in making her do just as I wished."

Excerpt from *The Story of My Life*
by Helen Keller

This book is dedicated to M. T.,
Miriam Therese Winter,
who more than once helped me keep
singing in the dark,
with my love.

The Mistress's Bell

Martha and her mother were in the cookhouse shelling peas when Ella stuck her head in the door.

"Sadie, she's got company coming," she said.

A moment later, the mistress's bell rang and Sadie Washington gave a big sigh.

Martha grinned. Mama sure did hate having to leave a job half done.

When Mrs. Keller rang that bell, though, she meant Mama to drop everything and come on the double to find out what she wanted.

Martha's grin changed to a scowl. "Why's she always in such a rush?" she asked.

Her mother's only answer was a quick shake of her head. She bundled up the peapods in a tea towel and set them on the table. When she had hoisted herself onto her feet, she untied her apron, mopped the sweat off her face and shook the wrinkles out of her skirt.

When she stood still for a moment to gather her strength, Martha saw how tired she looked.

"I'll finish those, Mama," she said. She pulled the bundle over to her side of the table.

As she unwrapped it, her mother smiled and straightened her shoulders.

"Good girl," she said softly. Then she added, in a much brisker voice, "But don't you go skedaddling out of here if I'm not back when you're done. I'll be wanting you to help me with the laundry."

It was Martha's turn to sigh. She'd hoped to escape from the hot kitchen while her mother was gone. Why couldn't Ella or Viney lend a hand so she could get away long enough to visit the kittens in the stable?

Avoiding her mother's gaze, she bent her head and picked up a peapod.

Sadie's smile returned as Martha deftly split the pod open and popped the row of peas into the waiting saucepan.

Then the bell jangled again, loud and long. Clearly Mrs. Keller was annoyed at being kept waiting. Without another word, Martha's mother sped away.

"Poor Mama," Martha murmured and popped a handful of peas into her mouth. They were so sweet! She longed to help herself to more, but her mother

would be sure to notice. She got back to work. But she was not half done when Sadie Washington reappeared. She sank back down on her chair.

"Bless me, this kitchen is hotter than Hades!" she exclaimed, fanning her face with her open hand. Then she turned to Martha. "It's you she wants, sugar," she said. "She has a new lady friend coming. She needs you to keep Helen from making a scene while the visitor's here."

Martha did not lift her head. Why must the mistress always count on her to keep Helen out of the way at such times? It had been easy watching over Helen, even if she was deaf and blind, in the beginning. Martha was three years older and at first she had been taller than Helen. But Helen had sprouted up until now she and Martha were almost the same height. Helen was sturdier, too.

Martha longed to refuse to go. When Helen was in a rage, she was wild, hitting or pinching whoever tried to control her. Martha bent her head, picked another peapod and split it, pretending she had not understood. Mama was not fooled, though.

"No more dawdling, missy," she snapped. "You get a move on." Then she reached up to a nearby shelf and, taking down two fried cakes dusted with sugar,

4

handed them to Martha. "If Helen gives you trouble, you can sweeten her with these," she said. "Now you hustle. She's in the front garden."

As soon as Martha was a safe distance from the cookhouse, she stopped to eat one of the doughnuts. She was licking the last morsel of sugar off her fingers when Helen's old setter, Belle, came to meet her, tail waving, eyes pleading.

Martha grinned. "Oh, all right," she said softly, sharing the second doughnut with the dog. "This one was for Helen, but she'll never know." It was gone in a flash.

Hoping for more, Belle padded after her. They were halfway down the walk when Percy came flying toward them.

"Come see the kittens, Martha," he said. "Ezra says their eyes are open."

Martha glowered at him. She longed to go, but she shook her head. "I have to watch Helen," she muttered.

"Too bad," Percy said and took off again. He turned a cartwheel, then called back, "Why not bring her with you? Nobody would mind."

Martha didn't answer. He and she both knew Helen's mother wouldn't want her to be seen playing in the stable when the mistress had company.

Then, as Percy rounded the corner of the cookhouse, Martha heard her mother calling him to fetch her a bucket of water. She laughed.

"She's caught Percy, too," she told Belle. "Not that pumping one pail of water will hold him up for long. Let's go, dog."

❧ 2 ❧

The Fire and the Feather

Still grouchy about having to tend to Helen, Martha started to go on down the path. It wasn't fair. There was Percy, free to go and play with the kittens, at least when his chores were done. But keeping Helen safe was a chore that never seemed to end.

"If it wasn't for her starting that fire," she said to Belle, "*I* could be playing with Percy right now. I know she didn't do it on purpose, but it sure changed everything."

Recalling that nightmare afternoon, she slowed down for a minute. Her life had been so different in those old days. Then, she had not spent much time with the white folks. Helen was the pet of the house, while she, Martha, was just the cook's girl, spending her days with Mama in the kitchen or doing farm chores with the other children who lived on the Ivy Green plantation.

She smiled, remembering some of the mischief she and Percy had gotten into back then.

Small, golden-haired Helen had lived in a world apart from theirs. She had been adored by her mother and looked after by Viney or Ella, who washed, dressed and fed her when Mrs. Keller was busy.

Once she recovered from the horrible fever that had left her without sight or hearing, Helen had toddled about on her own. Whenever she bumped into something or fell, which was often, there was always someone ready to rush to pick her up and comfort her. She always wanted to get down, though, and hardly ever cried . . . until the fire.

Martha stood still as her memory replayed that scene. She'd been coming down the hall when she heard Ella cry out, then the sound of running feet. Racing to the door of the front room, she had glimpsed Helen with her apron and her hair in flames. Then Viney had dashed past and flung a blanket around Helen, wrapping her tightly from head to heel to smother the flames. She covered the burning hair, too, and muffled Helen's terrified sobs as she rolled her, still swaddled, across the carpet.

When Mrs. Keller came running and reached for Helen, Viney held her back. "Them burns got to be covered before they're touched," she said.

Nobody argued. Viney was the one who knew about such things. Martha saw her pat the mistress on her back as though she were the one who was hurt.

"What happened?" Mrs. Keller gulped, crouching close to her daughter.

"I think she must have spilled water onto her pinafore," Viney said. "Then maybe she was trying to dry the wet place. She doesn't understand fires are dangerous, Ma'am."

Martha had backed away then, her hands clamped over her mouth to keep from screaming. Poor, poor Helen!

At last, the doctor arrived and put salve on the burns and cut away Helen's shrivelled ringlets.

"You owe a debt of thanks to whoever put out that fire," he told Helen's mother. "Her speed not only saved Helen's life, but kept the burns from going deep. You must make sure from now on that someone watches over the child every minute, or the next time she does something like this, she might not survive."

The entire household had talked of nothing else for days afterward. Helen's golden hair was burnt black and her fair eyelashes had been charred so badly that they were now only stiff little black sticks. Her hands were also scorched, but the burns were not so deep that they would leave scars.

They tried to keep Helen out of danger after that, but she hated being made to stay still. Her mother did her best to guard her every minute, but it was impossible. That was when Mama had mentioned that her Martha might be trusted to keep Helen safe when Mrs. Keller could not spare the time.

Next thing Martha knew, she had been given the job. And here it was, years later, and she *still* had it. That was why Percy was playing with kittens while she was stuck minding Helen.

When she and Belle reached the front garden and she saw Helen sitting cross-legged on the lawn, Martha's resentment fell away. As she and the dog approached, Helen reached out and took something out of the grass and waved it excitedly over her head.

"She's found a feather," Martha told Belle. Since Helen often fed the hens, she knew all about feathers, but no chicken had any as large and straight as this.

"It must have come from a hawk," Martha murmured, hunkering down to see what Helen would do with her discovery. Helen had never been able to watch other children playing with their toys — not since that fever, at least. Yet this never seemed to stop her from inventing interesting and unexpected games of her own. Sometimes, not understanding how a plaything worked, she had upset people by calmly destroying their gifts. But Martha thought that the feather might be perfect. She heard Percy whistling on his way to the stable, but ignored him as she waited to see what Helen would do next.

First Helen drew the tip of the feather across her wrist and up and down her inner arm. She shivered with pleasure as it tickled her skin. After repeating this a few times, she stroked the tip down the bridge of her nose. She then sniffed at it. That made her sneeze. Both girls laughed.

Even though she can't see it, Martha thought, she sure is having herself a dandy time playing with it.

Helen ran her fingertips along the feather's soft edge. Finally she put it between her lips and tasted it. As she went on to bite the shaft, Mrs. Keller and her visitor came out of the house.

"Oh, here's Helen," Mrs. Keller said, smiling.

Martha understood why she was pleased. So often

Helen's face was blank or angry, but right now, with the sun shining on her curls and her whole being caught up in the feather, she looked like any other happy little girl.

She's doing her mama proud, Martha thought. Then, as she rose, she noticed the visitor was frowning. What was wrong? Helen looked pretty, and right now she was not making strange noises or waving her hands about, the way she often did.

"She shouldn't be putting that feather in her mouth," the woman declared. Before either of the others could say a word, she leaned down and spoke to Helen directly. "Let me have that dirty thing, sweetheart," she said, plucking the feather out of Helen's fingers and tossing it aside.

The mistress's hands knotted into fists.

"Helen can't see or hear, Miss Temple," she said. "I thought you would have heard."

Miss Temple stumbled back a few steps, her face reddening. "I'm sorry . . ." she started. "I wasn't told . . ."

But her apology broke off as Helen lunged forward, grabbing for her feather. When her wildly searching hands found neither the feather nor the stranger who had snatched it away from her, her face went scarlet and she gave a wordless cry.

Martha sucked in her breath. For the mistress's sake, she longed to keep the storm from breaking, but she knew it was already too late.

Helen flung herself face down on the grass and started to howl. She kicked the ground and pounded on it with clenched fists. Then she buried her face in her arms.

The visitor watched her in disbelief. Mrs. Keller winced and faced away for a moment.

Then Martha moved to shield Helen from the stranger's fascinated stare. Mrs. Keller sent Martha a quick smile and started to lead her company away.

Miss Temple glanced back at the girls and then asked in a quavering voice that infuriated Martha, "But, Mrs. Keller, is it safe to leave the poor child alone . . ."

Martha choked. What on earth would the mistress say to *that*?

"Of course. Martha is completely trustworthy," Mrs. Keller snapped. "She knows how to calm Helen down. Please, come along."

She did not pause, but strode on with Miss Temple scurrying to catch up with her.

The minute they were out of sight, Martha ran to

snatch up the feather and slip it under Helen's flying fist. Helen's cries broke off instantly. She sat up and, clutching her treasure, thrust it under her bottom.

Martha did laugh at that. Then she swiftly gathered a small bunch of flowers and put them in Helen's hand. She knew that a good way to distract Helen after an outburst like that was to present her with something unexpected . . . and if that didn't work, to back out of reach before Helen hit her or struck Belle. If the old dog was the unlucky one, she just lowered her head and waited for Helen to stop twisting her ears or kicking her. Then, head hanging, she would move a safe distance away.

Martha always did her best to dodge the flailing fists, for if one of Helen's blows connected, she knew she must not hit back, no matter how much she wanted to. After all, she was just the cook's child. Helen was not only a Keller, but the daughter of the house, and besides, she had enough problems already.

This time, the flowers did the trick. Once Helen had smelled the blossoms, Martha picked some more and, letting Helen feel what she was doing, started making them into a chain. Belle had watched them until Helen settled. Then she sighed, waved her tail and stretched out nearby.

Helen soon pulled the feather out from under herself and thrust it deep into her pocket. Then she jumped up and, catching hold of Martha's elbow, steered her over to the porch of the cottage they called the Little House.

Martha was pleased to go along. It would be much cooler sitting under the honeysuckle vines and ivy that twined around the porch pillars, and the two of them would be hidden away there.

Helen's battered rag doll, Nancy, had been left out on the porch. Helen, discovering her, plumped her up to be used as a pillow and stretched out on the wide step.

Martha smiled. That old raggedy doll was homely, but soft and nice to hug. Besides, if Helen was resting, keeping an eye on her would be easy.

Martha grinned, remembering what Helen had done to the other rag doll that her Aunt Evelyn had made for her. It had been soft, too, but the front of its head had been left blank. Her other dolls had button eyes or embroidered ones that she could feel. Helen had pawed at its blank face, clearly unhappy with it, and when nobody understood, she had finally yanked beads off her aunt's cloak and placed them where the doll's eyes should be.

"I believe she wants her doll to have *eyes*," Aunt Evelyn had exclaimed, delighted to have realized what Helen was after.

She had hurried to sew the beads on. Helen had been pleased, but a day or two later she had discarded that doll and gone back to rocking Nancy. Everyone had been surprised by this, but Martha had figured that Helen just wanted that doll to have a face like her other dolls.

Martha settled on the porch above Helen. From there, she spotted Ella carrying a tray of cool drinks and macaroons across to the mistress and her guest, seated under the trees behind the Big House. Martha caught enough of their talk to know that the mistress was telling Miss Temple all about the dreadful illness Helen had had when she was not quite two.

Helen had gone to sleep now, her eyes closed and one of her golden curls falling across her rosy cheek. She was the picture of peace. It was hard to believe she could ever be wild with anger.

Martha yawned and tried to stop listening to the mistress. After all, she knew the story by heart. She could even dimly remember the family's grief when, after Helen's terrible fever was gone, they realized that she had lost her sight and then her hearing.

"Before her illness," Mrs. Keller was saying, "she was such a bright little thing. She started walking on her first birthday, and she had begun to talk. She'd hold up her cup and say 'wawa' until Martha or Ella filled it for her."

It was true. Martha could remember that well enough, but also, after the sickness, Helen struggling to be free of the hands that held her. In no time she was bumping into furniture or falling down steps, never seeming to learn she was in danger. Then she had set herself on fire and Martha had been stuck with watching over her.

Martha was so lost in thought that she almost missed catching sight of Percy sliding toward her, his back flattened against the wall, his body hidden by the flowers. Careful not to disturb Helen's sleep, she rose to watch him. What was he clutching and why was he choking down laughter?

Then she saw the tiny kitten held snug against his chest. "Oooh, Percy," she whispered, reaching out to stroke the kitten's head.

It let out a shrill mew loud enough to break the stillness. When Martha swung around, Miss Temple was craning her neck, staring over in their direction. Martha sniffed. Trust her not to miss a thing.

"Go before you get caught, Percy," she hissed.

Percy winked at her and took off, moving as silently as a shadow.

Martha giggled and sat back down.

More and more often, since the fire, Mrs. Keller had brought Helen out to the cookhouse. Always Martha's mother would make both of them welcome. While Helen toddled around their feet, her mother would sometimes pour out her fears to Sadie Washington. It's almost as though she needs someone to listen who's not family, Martha had decided. For although Captain Keller doted on his little Helen, he was frequently stern and impatient with his wife.

Those were the times that you could almost count on the mistress showing up in the kitchen soon afterward. After she'd left, Martha's mother would shake her head and murmur, "That poor soul."

"The mistress isn't poor," Martha objected finally.

"Her folks are hard on her. That's all I mean," her mother had answered. "You keep a still tongue in your head now and take Helen outdoors for a bit to give her mama a break."

Wonder how Mama manages to get on with her work and listen to the mistress's troubles and laugh at Ella's jokes and almost never lose her temper, Martha thought. Mama was not like anyone else.

Back then, Martha had been pleased as punch to be given the job. It got her out of some chores, and keeping an eye on a toddler hadn't been too hard. Now, though—

Miss Temple's voice suddenly broke into Martha's thoughts. "How dreadful for you! Surely something can be done to help such a case."

"Dr. Bell — you know of Alexander Graham Bell, I'm sure; he is interested in the deaf — is finding us a teacher," Helen's mother replied. "He is sure Helen can be helped. I just pray the teacher will come soon."

Martha knew Mama prayed the same prayer. "That poor mite is in prison, Martha," she had said. "You and that old dog are the only company she has. She needs you to be her friend."

Martha often wished her mother would stop talking about how lonely Helen must be and how Martha must be her friend. She tried getting Mama to understand. "How can you make friends with somebody who doesn't *hear* what you say or *see* things you try to show her? I do what she wants, Mama, but she is *always* the boss. Being friends is different."

Mama would shake her head, but Martha knew what she said was true. "Helen *always* gets her own way, and never gets punished, no matter if she hits Belle or me," she told Mama. "How can you be friends with someone who hurts you on purpose?"

She knew she was right. After all, Percy was a pest lots of times, but he was her friend and he would never do such mean things.

She sighed and slapped at a mosquito. "Just once I wish somebody besides Percy would take *my* side," she whispered, snuggling up to Belle. No matter how hard Helen hit or pinched her, it was always Helen that people felt sorry for.

Even when Helen bit her and she showed her mother the teeth marks on her arm, Mama just told Martha to stop fussing over nothing. Martha knew that this was partly because her mother needed to keep her job. She had come to Ivy Green with the mistress when she'd married the Captain, and if the Captain ever took it into his head that he wanted another cook, she and Martha would have to leave Ivy Green. The mistress might argue, but her husband was the boss. So Martha knew why Mama had to watch her step, and why *she* had to put up with all Helen's outbursts in silence.

Percy had been shocked when he saw the bite marks, though. *He* had not called it nothing.

Maybe that teacher would make the difference,

Martha decided. Her spirits lifted. The teacher was bound to be shocked by Helen's tantrums. Maybe she would actually find a way to force Helen to behave herself.

All at once, Martha was fed up with sitting still. She wanted to be playing with those kittens, not stuck here at the house. She sighed and slapped at another mosquito, then pulled the feather out of Helen's pocket and began to tickle her arm with it. Although she couldn't take Helen to the stable until the visitor left, in case she made a rumpus crossing the garden, she could start waking her up.

The minute Miss Temple's carriage disappeared, Martha sprang up, snatched Helen's hand and started to tow her out to the stable. Helen dragged her feet to begin with, but as soon as she realized where Martha was heading, she came along eagerly.

"Wait until you meet the kittens," Martha said. She knew other people thought she was silly to chatter away when Helen could not hear, but Martha needed to talk to her. If she didn't, Helen would somehow seem more like a thing than a person.

Helen loved the kittens, just as Martha had known she would. It was hard to make her be gentle with their small, squirming bodies, though. She did not

understand that she must not grip them too tightly. The kittens defended themselves with their pinprick paws.

When Helen got a genuine scratch, Martha moved like lightning to rescue the innocent little tabby from her clutch.

Helen did her best to snatch the kitten back, but Martha set it out of reach in the hay and hauled Helen back to the house. It was too bad that Helen so often spoiled the fun by not understanding what was happening. Martha remembered all too vividly the day when Helen had squeezed a baby chick and Martha had not rescued it quickly enough to save its life.

"Why don't you ever learn?" she muttered, tugging Helen down the path to the Big House and handing her over to her mother, then running off before the mistress could notice the tiny scratches the kittens had made on the back of Helen's hand.

Feeling miserable without knowing why, Martha headed back to the cookhouse. Her mother was not there when she arrived, but Martha's bad mood melted away when she spotted the clean laundry on the table, all folded and sorted into neat piles — *her* job, but Mama had done it. "Thank you, Mama," she said and started back out the door. Then she stopped to help herself to a drink of water and a piece of cornbread. She was too hot to go back to the stable. What's more, she was hungry. She sat down and began to eat and drink before she was sent to do some new chore. It was still hot in the kitchen, although a breeze was rustling the trees as the afternoon drew in.

She looked at the clean clothes and knew that her mother would soon be sending her to put them away. Maybe she should give Mama a surprise and do it before she returned.

As she picked up a pile of underclothes and stockings, she could hear Helen wailing about something, but who could tell what it might be? Helen's Aunt Evelyn would have just said, "Helen can't even think." But Martha didn't believe that. Helen *did* know things. She had petted the kitten, and her hands must know how it felt — its wriggle, its tiny tail, its baby ears. All she didn't know was that it was a kitten. It was only the *word* she was missing.

Her *fingers* know things, but she doesn't know those things have *names*, Martha thought.

Martha took the pile of clothes and ran to the family's living quarters. She was at the back porch as her mother returned down the path. She paused, listening, to hear whether Mama would notice the things she had taken.

"Martha, where are you?" Sadie Washington called softly.

Martha grinned and sped up to deliver the clean clothes to the bureau drawers in the bedrooms. When she came back outside, her mother was standing at the cookhouse door with another armful. She smiled and held them out.

"Thought I'd give the good fairy a helping hand," she said.

Martha took the bundle and went back, laughing softly. As she reached the Big House, she remembered what she had been thinking about Helen, who was now clearly laughing at something.

Words, she thought, as she put away the clothes. That's all she's missing. But they matter. You can *feel* things, but without words you can't *tell* anybody what you're feeling. But how will the teacher give her words?

Birthday

Weeks went by and still the teacher failed to appear.

The mistress burst into the kitchen one morning with tears spilling down her cheeks. Martha backed into the corner beside the woodstove and huddled down, out of sight. Then she strained to hear what was troubling Helen's mother now.

"Oh, Sadie, Helen's going to turn six next week and she doesn't even know it will be her birthday. Her father thinks I'm being silly, but it breaks my heart to look at her and not be able to explain things to her . . ." Mrs. Keller wept.

"I'll make her a cake fit for a queen," Martha's mother said at once.

"But she won't even *know* . . ." Mrs. Keller moaned.

"Never you mind, Ma'am. That little one loves cake. You see if she doesn't gobble down six whole slices," Sadie Washington said.

Helen certainly did love the birthday cake. By the time she had finished her third slice, she was covered with icing from ear to ear — her face slathered all over with white icing, her ringlets sticky with it.

But Martha also saw how Helen was beginning to notice that she was different from the people around her. She'd try to take part in things the rest of them were doing, but did not know how. Over and over, either Ella or Martha was told to take her away so the other family members could have some peace. Martha had to get help now that Helen had grown so strong, but even then, when they tried, Helen would dig in her heels and screech and strike out at whoever was trying to lead her away. It would end with them having to haul her up the stairs or outside. When Martha struggled to hold on to her hand, she would twist Martha's fingers or bend them backwards. Every time Helen's shoe slammed into one of Martha's shins, it seemed to be shouting, "why?" over and over again! *Why, why, why?*

If only there was a way to make things clear to Helen, Martha thought. But there wasn't. You needed words.

The mistress took to spending even more time in the cookhouse, spilling out her worries. Martha wondered why until one day her mother said, "That poor lady. She's so alone."

Martha was confused — what did Mama mean? The house was *full* of people. There was Helen and her parents and her much older half-brother James, plus her Aunt Evelyn. And there were relatives who came and went.

Ella and Viney spent most of their daytime hours helping out inside the Big House, too. Martha and her mother were always nearby. And there were men who looked after the animals and the crops and gardens — though the mistress didn't see as much of them. And even though there were whispers about the Captain having lost money during the war, he was forever bringing home guests to dinner or to go hunting.

Anyway, Martha decided, how could Helen's mother be lonely when she was so often inviting people like Miss Temple over? She couldn't.

One afternoon Martha was feeding the hens in the yard when she heard Mrs. Keller arrive in the cookhouse. As usual, she was upset. Martha crouched outside the open window, ready to eavesdrop as usual. She went stiff when she heard the mistress burst out that some of the family were urging her and the Captain to send Helen away. "They think she belongs in an asylum for mental *defectives*!" Mrs. Keller moaned.

Martha herself had actually heard James mutter something of the kind when Helen had been particularly destructive, but she had not believed such a thing would really happen. After all, Helen was definitely not slow-witted. When Mama taught her to help cook something, Helen copied her hand motions exactly and could do it again later without a single mistake. When she was small, she had often got herself lost, but not any longer. She knew her way around the Ivy Green grounds, especially the lovely garden that surrounded the house. She could even go upstairs and fetch something the mistress wanted.

"James keeps insisting she should be put away, and even the Captain once said she might be happier with her 'own kind,'" Helen's mother sobbed.

Who were Helen's "own kind"? Martha wondered, holding her breath so she could hear how Mama would respond.

"Your Helen's some sharp — sharp as a tack," Sadie Washington snapped. "Don't you pay them no mind, Ma'am. If Helen could see and hear, she'd soon show them how quick she is."

A pan rattled. Martha grinned, remembering what

a mess Helen had made of herself while they were working on the cake just this morning. Helen, angry at not being allowed to stir the batter, had shoved the big bowl off the table, sending the contents splattering everywhere. Ella had dodged so fast she managed not to get covered with the stuff. Then, glaring at Helen, she had started cleaning up the floor.

Martha's mother had gone for a rag to wipe off what had splashed onto her skirt and to clean Helen off, but before she could, Helen had leaned way forward and begun sucking the batter off her bare *toes*. When her busy tongue tickled her, she started giggling and everyone else joined in. Mama had ended up bent double, and Martha had laughed so hard she cried.

Captain Keller wouldn't have thought it was funny, Martha decided, that was for sure.

"The servants are not like us," she had heard him telling his wife the week before. "You should stop Helen spending so much time with them in that cookhouse."

"I can't keep her with me every minute of the day, Captain. You try minding her without a break for a bit, and you might understand better," she had said in a weary voice.

"Don't be ridiculous," he had roared. "Caring for

the child is not a man's job. You know perfectly well I'm far too busy."

Martha had hoped to hear more, but that had been the end.

Mama was right about Helen being smart, though. If she wasn't smart, she wouldn't have made up so many ways to tell them things. Not in words, of course. Yet Helen had invented many gestures. She shook her head for No and nodded for Yes. She made spectacles with her fingers to represent her father. She stroked her cheek or pulled at the back of her hair to mean her mother, who usually wore her hair in a bun. When she wanted bread, she acted out cutting a slice and buttering it. Her meaning was plain to anyone who watched her.

Glancing up from her hiding place, Martha saw Helen's father striding down the drive. If Helen had known he was near, she would have run to him. With everyone else, he was rough and demanding, but he was always gentle with Helen. He would take her out into his garden and let her feel the blossoms and smell their fragrance. He would feed her a strawberry or a grape, laughing as he popped it into her open mouth.

He seemed to be a different person when he was spending time with Helen. Just a couple of weeks ago, he had led her to a guinea hen's nest hidden in the long grass and shown her how to carry it, cupped in her two hands, into the cookhouse.

The next afternoon, Helen had caught Martha's arm and, bending down, made a nest shape with her two hands. Then she had led Martha into the long grass to search. Before long, the two of them had located another nest. Very pleased with herself, Helen had borne her find to the cookhouse to present to Martha's mother. She had done this several times now.

The only problem was, even when *Martha* was the one who found the hidden nest, Helen insisted that she hand it over. Martha hated it when Helen took the nests away and marched off to deliver them. She wished Helen would trip and let the nest fall to the ground.

But she'd got her revenge. Just the day before, she had spotted a nest and not let Helen know. Later on, when the Captain had taken Helen out in the carriage, Martha had run back, got the eggs and presented them to her mother.

Sadie Washington had shaken her head, but she had kept Martha's secret.

Martha couldn't help grinning at having tricked Helen for once. Maybe she *should* feel ashamed, but she *didn't*.

Percy startled Martha out of her thoughts as he and his little sister Minta came running toward her hiding place.

"Where's Helen gone?" Percy whispered. "We were supposed to be minding her for a minute, but we lost her. Martha, find her quick."

Martha didn't stop to ask where they had last seen Helen, but followed them out into the front garden, where she might be crouched down behind one of the boxwood hedges. Martha strained her ears as she looked everywhere she could think of. She scurried around the garden and finally stopped under a tree Helen loved. She peered up. Blossoms came fluttering down on top of her head.

Then she heard whimpering sounding from the tree branches above.

"Percy, she's here," she called softly. "Come and help me get her down."

Percy climbed the tree as nimbly as a squirrel while Martha and Minta watched. Helen had both arms wrapped around the tree's trunk, afraid to let go. Percy reached out to touch her and then pulled back his hand, not wanting to startle her.

Martha stiffened. What if Helen slipped? Calling to her would not help, of course. And they had to act fast. Minta was getting ready to howl and give them away.

"You *hush*," Martha hissed at her. Then, "Come down, Percy. I'll get her. Just be ready to help catch her if she falls."

Martha was not as quick and nimble as Percy, but when she drew near Helen, she reached out and gently bounced the limb where Helen was perched, to let her know someone was there.

Helen let go and swung to face her, and was about to topple down when Martha grabbed hold of her. She held on with all her strength.

Below them, Percy started to beam.

"I'm coming down with her. Be ready to help," Martha told him. Helen flung her arms around Martha, almost knocking her off balance, but Martha had wrapped her legs around the trunk and managed to keep her grip as she eased herself and Helen down. At least Helen wasn't that far up the tree. And at least it was filled with blossoms and not thorns. In only a few moments they were back on the ground.

"Thank the Lord she can't tell anyone we lost her," Percy whispered, backing away from the scene and pulling Minta after him.

His eyes were shining. Martha had to laugh. She

had often thought the same thing. She reached out and brushed the blossoms off Helen's head and shoulders and led her back to the cookhouse.

Mama looked at their flushed faces and shook her head. "I won't ask," she said. "Help yourself to a cookie and take her out to see those kittens the two of you are so fond of."

A few days later, Martha went out to Helen's tree and, when nobody was nearby, climbed into the fragrant, flowery branches on her own. It was lovely there, perched high in the midst of the blooming tree. No one would notice her, but she had the world stretched out beneath her. It was magical.

Percy ran past and she grinned, peering down at the top of his head without his even guessing she was there. She opened her mouth to call to him, and then did not. A breeze blew through the tree and she felt drenched in its fragrance. What a perfect place for an escape.

A week later, Martha was following Helen out to the cookhouse when both of them stopped to draw in the scent of freshly baked sponge cake. Martha gazed at the cake itself, set out to cool on the table. While she licked her lips, Helen leaped forward and stretched out her hands to feel for the cake.

Martha gasped as Helen picked up the cake pan and started for the open door.

"*No!* You can't take that!" Martha managed, running after her. "Mama will skin you alive."

But Helen was in the yard and heading away like a runaway pony. She reached the woodpile and hid behind it, the cake still clutched against herself. Once she was sitting down, she began digging out chunks of it with greedy fingers.

Martha could not believe what she was seeing. When half of the cake had vanished, Helen stopped, pulled out a smaller bit and held it out in Martha's direction.

Martha stayed frozen in place. Helen made a grunting sound and waved the piece around, clearly wanting Martha to take it. She was trying to share! Helen had never offered to share *anything* she was eating before. Martha hesitated, but when Helen made another impatient sound, she took the piece of cake and ate it. Meanwhile, Helen had finished what was left and thrown the cake pan behind the woodpile. It landed in plain sight.

Martha decided to get rid of the evidence, and then was afraid she would be spotted hiding the pan. She took Helen's hand and pulled her around the side of the house, into the front garden.

"Just wait until they miss that cake," she muttered. Then she drew Helen behind the boxwood hedge and wiped the smeared crumbs off her mouth and dress with some leaves.

By suppertime, Helen was sick. Since Martha had eaten only the one piece of cake, she was fine. Not for the first time, she was pleased that Helen could not tattle. When she heard Helen retching, she was glad she had been given such a stingy chunk.

Haircut

One afternoon in late June, Martha came out to the porch and discovered Helen with a pair of scissors in her hand. She was clearly fascinated by them, snapping the blades open and shut. Martha backed up a step and stood stock still, watching Helen try to figure out how the scissors worked.

Helen proceeded to snip off a honeysuckle flower, then another and another. Then she began awkwardly cutting through the laces that did up her boots.

Martha gasped. Blossoms were one thing. Laces were another. Doing her best not to attract Helen's attention, she reached for the scissors. The mistress would want her to stop Helen from destroying those laces. But she couldn't catch hold of them — not the way Helen was waving them around. "I do wish you could *hear*," she muttered, watching the laces come apart. "You're going to get me in a pile of trouble."

At last, she started to turn to go for help when Helen reached out and caught hold of her arm, and then leaned over and grabbed her hair and pulled at it.

"Hey, quit that!" Martha yelled, trying to jerk free. But before she could escape, Helen had managed to snip off the curl she had hold of. Without pausing, she tried to snip off more of the corkscrew curls Mama had tied with bits of yarn.

"No, Helen!" Martha shrieked, yanking hard now. She could not believe Helen was actually going to keep at it.

But Helen went right on. The wild way she kept swinging the scissors around made dodging too dangerous. After all, Helen could not see where the blades were slicing. Any minute, one might plunge into Martha, gouging a hole in her cheek or her eye.

Martha shut her eyelids tight and covered her face with her free arm. She screamed again, as loudly as she could, even though she was sure nobody was within earshot.

"Please, Helen, *please!*" she begged. But Helen's grip was like iron and she was shrieking with laughter as curl after curl fell from Martha's head. By now Martha was sobbing, tears pouring down her face. Yet Helen didn't slow down or even seem to notice. Most of Martha's tight curls now lay heaped on the ground.

Fury blazed up inside her. The next instant, she wrenched the scissors out of Helen's hand. "I'll show you!" she shouted.

Without hesitating, she cut off one of Helen's long golden ringlets.

She was glaring at Helen and clutching the curl when Mrs. Keller came bustling onto the porch. She stared for one horrified second, unable to believe her eyes, while Martha stayed frozen.

"Oh no!" Mrs. Keller wailed. She caught Helen in her arms and held her close, while staring at Martha's head. Most of her hair had been hacked off, although there were still some ragged tufts left.

Martha, with the scissors and the single bright ringlet still clutched in her fist, knew she should say she was sorry and look ashamed, but *she* had not been the one to start the wickedness. What's more, she was neither sorry nor ashamed. She gritted her teeth and stood her ground.

Mrs. Keller dropped her gaze before she spoke. "You have to forgive her, Martha," she half-whispered. "She doesn't know she's doing wrong."

Martha opened her mouth to yell, "She does *so!*" But she bit back the words. Surely the mistress could see for herself that Helen was laughing fit to burst.

Martha dropped the scissors and the curl and took to her heels. When she reached the kitchen, she flung herself into Mama's arms and let loose the storm of sobs she had been holding back.

Sadie Washington stared at Martha's shorn head and the tears streaming down her face. Then she gave Martha a tight hug. "Honey-lamb, I just made icing for their cake. *You* shall get to lick the spoon," she said.

This was a treat she always saved for Helen.

Martha's sobs subsided a little . . . but it still didn't make up for what Helen had done to her.

"Mama, she . . . she . . ." She fought to get the words out but her mother broke in.

"I know, I know. But it's over now. I have a kerchief you can wear," her mother said, stroking Martha's back while the crying grew less. "Your hair will grow back. I promise."

Martha wished Mama would rush to tell Helen's mother how badly she had been hurt, but she knew it would not happen. Mama had explained many times that it wasn't wise to complain about Helen. All the same, she was comforted by the anger in her mother's voice. She buried her face in Mama's chest and, after one last sniff, made herself stop weeping.

When Percy spotted her, even with her head hidden under Mama's scarf, he danced about, pointed his finger at her and squealed, "Baldy, baldy. You look like a melon."

Martha went at him, her hands scratching away his grin.

"Don't you *dare* call me names," she threatened, "or I'll tell Jacob." Of all the older boys on the plantation, Jacob was the one the younger ones feared. Martha steered clear of him, but she knew he was mean.

"I won't say another word," Percy promised.

But she could see the laughter he was choking back.

She forgave him totally, though, when she heard him warning Minta not to make fun of her. "Poor Martha," he said. "It's not her fault nobody makes that Helen behave herself."

Martha had to endure plenty more teasing, though, even though Percy did chase a bunch of the younger boys away when they came dancing after her, whispering about her hair.

Martha knew some of the mocking was because she was always indoors with Helen and her family. She wasn't made to work in the fields or help with the barn chores. Mama sometimes slipped her a special treat, too, when she gave one to Helen. Martha understood how the other children on the plantation felt, but it still hurt when they called her "Baldy."

Her mother's scarf covered her head, but everyone knew how her hair looked. She did not say so, but inwardly she raged at Helen for putting her in such a fix. For a few days, Martha did her best to make herself scarce, even when she knew Helen was trying to find her.

Sometimes she wondered whether Helen had any idea how deeply she had hurt her. Did Helen understand that she had made Martha almost totally bald? She could not hear the other children's taunts, of course, but didn't she guess? The only way to tell her would be to take Helen's hand and force it to feel her bare scalp.

I ought to do it, Martha told herself.

But she couldn't.

Finally, she let go of her grudge. Hard as it was to believe, Helen really did not seem to take in what she had done. The very day after it happened, she had come back out to the cookhouse as happily as ever.

Whenever Mrs. Keller noticed the scarf covering Martha's shorn scalp, she shook her head and repeated how sorry she believed Helen would be if she understood what she had done. Martha did not respond at first, but Mrs. Keller seemed so sad that finally Martha could not stand it any longer and nodded as though she, too, believed Helen had not acted deliberately.

In the days that followed, Martha noticed that Helen seemed afraid to come searching for her, no longer pawing the air until she found Martha's hand and grabbed hold of it. Now, when she touched Martha, she stood still and then backed away looking bewildered.

Yet Martha noticed that things were better once she stopped dwelling on the memory of what Helen had done.

Eventually her hair began to grow back and she was no longer a laughingstock. Her mother said her short soft curls looked fine and she could give up hiding her head with the kerchief. Although she still shrank when she thought the others might start teasing her again, Martha at last grew brave enough to look at herself in the big mirror in the mistress's room. She smiled as she saw that Mama had been telling the truth.

Then Sally, one of the older girls who came to help with housework sometimes, looked at Martha's soft curls and said, "Don't you worry about your hair, honey. Those curls look real sweet."

Martha ducked and ran away, but she was grinning.

Helen seemed to calm down in the next few weeks. Her father took her out for rides in the carriage more often and while she was gone, Ella began teaching Martha to knit. She learned fast, and as soon as she was ready to start on a proper project Ella suggested that she knit a baby blanket. It could have a fancy edge, but most of it would be straightforward and easy for her. Martha did not ask what baby would be given it if she ever got it finished. There were always babies being born somewhere on the Ivy Green plantation. Whenever she was not working on the blanket, she hid it away, afraid Helen might discover it and pull it apart trying to figure out what it was.

It almost seemed as if Helen was not being so bad now, until the day Martha came home from running an errand to find Helen sitting on the porch steps, stamping her feet and roaring with laughter.

"What have you done now?" Martha whispered, staring at her.

Then she heard. Within the house, someone was pounding and calling out for help. Martha started to dash inside to see what was going on, when she spotted a key lying on the step next to Helen. She snatched it up and raced in to open whatever door Helen might have locked. When she heard noises from inside the pantry, she ran and turned the key. The woman who emerged was unrecognizable. Helen's mother was always beautifully dressed and groomed. This woman was dishevelled, flushed and tear streaked. She staggered out and sank down on the nearest chair.

"I've been in there for *hours*," she wheezed, her voice hoarse from calling out for help. "Why didn't you come?"

"Mama went to town. Viney sent me on some errands. Nobody else is home," Martha whispered, sure she would be blamed. "We didn't hear you."

"What is Helen doing now?" Mrs. Keller asked wearily.

Martha gulped. How could she tell the mistress that Helen was outside, rocking back and forth, howling with laughter?

When Martha looked at the door to the porch but did not answer, Helen's mother glanced that way but stayed slumped on her chair.

"The teacher must come soon or we will all lose our minds," she said in a tired voice.

"I'll get you a drink," Martha mumbled, turning to run to the kitchen.

She got a tumbler from the shelf and dipped some water into it, then hurried back with it clutched in her hand.

"Thank you, child," the mistress said, taking the glass in hands that trembled.

Martha was trying not to stare, but she came to her senses in time to reach out and steady Mrs. Keller's shaking hand.

As Mrs. Keller took a sip and gave the glass back, Martha couldn't help wondering if Helen would be forgiven this time. Surely not. There was nowhere to sit in the pantry. The air must have been hot and dusty. It must have been horrible to be trapped in such a place. This time, Helen's trick was unpardonable. What if the mistress had needed the privy?

Martha choked back a giggle. It wasn't funny. Surely *this* time Helen would be in trouble.

She waited to see, but nothing happened. Every so often, she would catch the mistress looking at her, but neither of them spoke of what Helen had done that afternoon. It became a sort of secret they shared.

❦ 5 ❦

What Next?

After that day, Martha began to realize more of what Mama meant about Helen being a prisoner. Bit by bit, she was coming to see how alone Helen was and how powerless she must feel.

It worried Martha to see how Helen struggled to figure out what people were doing when they were having a conversation. She would stand between adults who were talking to each other above her and put up her hand to feel their moving lips. Then she tried her best to imitate them.

Sometimes the adults would laugh at her attempts. Maybe Helen couldn't tell, but Martha could. Didn't they see how Helen was struggling to make sense out of what they were doing? If Martha could manage it without seeming rude, she would take Helen's hand and draw her away, giving her something to hold and explore with her fingertips.

One day she caught Percy imitating Helen, then laughing at his own pantomime. "Don't you *do* that," she hissed.

"She's funny," he wailed.

"No, she *isn't*," Martha said. "Don't you tease her like that! Not when she's trying so hard." She ran off before Viney or Ella could come to Percy's defence.

But Percy's laughter was nothing compared to what came one afternoon when the Kellers were entertaining a crowd of friends and relatives. Martha was bringing in dishes of food just as Mrs. Keller and Helen's aunts came downstairs, in all their finery, to greet the arriving guests. Martha looked for Helen to follow them down, but she wasn't there. Helen must still be upstairs with Ella or Viney, she decided, until she spotted Helen starting down the stairs.

Martha froze and almost dropped the tray she was carrying.

Helen's face was slathered with cold cream. She wore her mother's motoring veil and had tied a bustle around her waist. She had on a pair of women's shoes, far too big for her. Martha couldn't stop staring. The way Helen moved down those stairs made it clear she was proud of what she had accomplished. She'd dressed up to greet the guests, just like her mother and aunts.

People laughed, shrieked, clapped and pointed at her bizarre get-up. Mrs. Keller followed their gaze and broke off her conversation in mid-sentence.

"Martha . . ." she managed.

Not sure what the mistress wanted her to do, Martha set down the tray, went over and took Helen by the hand. As Martha began removing Helen from what she seemed to regard as the scene of her triumph, the mistress looked relieved. Forcing Helen to leave was far from easy, but at last, Martha got her back up the stairs. She cleaned the goo off Helen's face while she fought to escape, and got the extra clothes and the shoes off her, too. Helen pinched and pulled away, battling with Martha as she so often did. Still, Martha could not help admiring what Helen had invented. Without being able to check her appearance in a mirror, she had done a good job of imitating her mother's and aunts' party attire. It was some accomplishment.

When Martha told her mother about it, giving all the details, Sadie Washington shook her head and then laughed so hard she had to sit down.

"The poor child has such a shock coming her way," she said. "I'm glad she's having some fun out of life while she still can."

Martha stared at her mother. What did she mean?

53

"Oh, Martha, surely you've noticed that we'll soon be having an addition to the Keller family," her mother said. Then she started to hum. Martha was mystified still until Sadie Washington added a few words. "When the bough breaks, the cradle will fall."

And at last, Martha caught on. Mrs. Keller must be expecting a baby.

⚘ 6 ⚘

Big Sister

Sadie Washington said nothing more for a few weeks, but after she had told Martha the news, she often talked about it with Ella and Viney when they collected in the kitchen for their morning tea. All of them were eager to discuss how Helen would react when she was presented with a little brother or sister. Martha joined them and sat silently listening as usual.

"Does she know what a baby is? I don't think she's ever held one," Viney said.

Martha wanted to speak up then. Helen would often put her doll Nancy into the tall cradle that had been her own bed when she was a baby. She would sit next to it and rock the old rag doll for an hour or more, making strange little grunting sounds as the cradle swung back and forth. Didn't that say that she knew what a baby was? Watching Helen with Nancy, Martha had sometimes felt a sadness she did not quite understand. It hurt her to hear the meaningless sounds Helen made, and she would find herself trying harder to befriend Helen. But this was never easy. Sometimes Helen seemed more bent on delivering pinches or sharp pushes directly after Martha had done her best to be kind.

But Martha wasn't about to say anything about that to Mama or Ella or Viney right now. The minute they noticed she was listening, they would be sure to send her off on some errand. And she wanted to listen. She stayed still and kept her face blank.

"I doubt Helen does know what a baby is," Sadie Washington said. "It's going to be some hard for her. She's never had to share her mother with any other child."

"That's a fact," Ella declared, helping herself to a biscuit. "Maybe it'll do her good."

"The mistress must be worried sick about it," Sadie Washington said slowly, moving the biscuit plate out of reach. "We'll just have to give Helen more attention." The other women laughed.

"I guess she'll soon find out she's not the only pebble on the beach," Ella said, tossing her head but lowering her voice. "I think it'll do that girl good to be put in her place for once."

Martha knew how cruelly Helen had mistreated Ella and understood why she sounded so hard-hearted when she talked about her, but still, she was troubled by the thought of Helen being hurt when the baby came.

As the time for the birth drew nearer, it was painful to watch Helen trying to get onto her mother's lap and finding that there was not enough room for her. Often she would run away and rock Nancy in her cradle.

If only they could explain the change that was coming, Martha thought. But nobody knew how to do it.

Now when Helen tried to climb onto her mother's knee, the mistress would heave herself out of the rocker and move to the sofa. There Helen could snuggle up next to her and be held. But Martha could see how confused Helen was by the change. What would happen when a live baby took the place that had been Helen's all her life?

Two or three times, Martha had seen the mistress place Helen's hand on her stomach to let her feel the baby move, but Helen always jerked her hand away. Finally she must have actually felt the unborn child kick, for she gave a cry and ran from the room, leaving her mother in tears.

When little Mildred Keller was born, the tension in the house soared. Family and servants alike did their best to make Helen love her baby sister. But what should have been a joyful time was more often upsetting. Mrs. Keller kept trying to help Helen accept Mildred, getting her to feel her new sister's small hand or even to sit and help to hold her. But Helen cried out and put her hands behind her back, or pulled free and ran from the room. It was clear that Helen saw her sister as an intruder, taking *her* place on her mother's lap and stealing the cherishing that had always been hers.

"Martha, you'll have to keep an even closer watch over Helen now," Mama said.

"Why?" Martha demanded, although she thought she guessed.

Martha's mother made the situation crystal clear. "The baby might not be safe if she's ever left alone with Helen," she said.

"Helen wouldn't really hurt her," Martha declared. But it was only a couple of days later that Helen ran over to the cradle where the baby was fast asleep and shoved the side of it hard enough to tip it. Mildred, still sleeping, slid to the edge and began to fall. Martha was not near enough to reach her, but Mrs. Keller was. She leaped up and caught the baby before she fell to the floor. "Helen must not have known Mildred was asleep there," Mrs. Keller whispered, holding her infant daughter close.

But Martha had seen the look on Helen's face. That shove she had given the baby's bed had been no accident, she told her mother.

"It wasn't my fault, Mama," she said. "I was on the far side of the room when the baby fell."

"I know that," her mother answered. "But you keep even more careful watch from now on, honey-lamb. Helen could hurt her sister without ever understanding what she did." After that, Martha shadowed Helen every waking minute. She had always been good at reading Helen's moods, but how could she be sure what Helen was planning?

"Oh, I do wish that teacher would hurry up and get here," she kept muttering whenever nobody was listening. "Please, hurry and come!"

7

Teacher

At long last, they got word that the teacher was on her way.

The night before she was to arrive, Martha lay awake, trying to imagine how life would be once Miss Annie Sullivan walked in the door.

Please, she prayed, let Helen behave. Let her not be too much for this Miss Sullivan to handle. Please.

The next morning, Helen seemed to pick up on the others' excitement. She ran upstairs and down, outside and in, never settling for longer than a minute. She kept going to the door, swinging it wide open, sweeping her hands through the empty space and then slamming the door shut, clearly disappointed to find only air. Martha longed to be able to tell Helen that she was right to expect someone, and who the newcomer would be.

"This whole household's on tenterhooks," Sadie

Washington whispered to Martha. The hours seemed twice as long as usual.

"You're right, Mama," Martha said. She'd seen Belle give a great sigh and meander out into the front hall, where she could lie down and still keep the door in sight. "Even Belle is jumpy."

When the carriage finally arrived, bringing Captain Keller and Miss Sullivan from the station, the Kellers and their servants were all taken aback. The teacher was so *small*, shorter than any grown woman they knew. She was also much younger than they had expected her to be, and her eyes were hidden behind dark glasses.

She explained right away that she needed to wear them because her eyes were sensitive to light, but Martha noticed the doubt, clear as day, on every face. Would such a tiny person be able to deal with Helen's frequent tantrums, her sudden shifts of moods, her fits of violence?

Helen's father was talking in an extra-loud voice, almost as though he thought the teacher didn't understand English. Martha wondered if it was because he didn't trust Yankees. Or because he was not partial to the Irish.

But Mrs. Keller took a deep breath and stepped

forward to welcome Annie Sullivan to their home. Martha figured she had waited far too long to give up without allowing Miss Annie a fair trial. If Dr. Bell had faith in her ability, surely she would prove to be the wonder worker they so desperately needed.

Martha, watching from the shadows, liked her at once. She was not nearly as tall as the mistress, for one thing. And she had a laugh that was as catching as a yawn.

When Miss Sullivan dropped her carpet bag to hug Helen, who was bouncing up and down with excitement, Martha slipped away to report to her mother how the first meeting had gone. "I like her laugh," she said. "I think she's going to be dandy."

"Praise the Lord," Sadie Washington replied.

Martha shot back to the Big House, just in time to see Helen diving into the teacher's valise and feeling around until she discovered a doll Miss Annie had brought her. Miss Annie explained to the Kellers that the doll had been dressed in clothing made especially for her by the children at the Perkins School for the Blind.

As Helen explored the lovely china doll's face and then felt its fancy dress, Martha's fingers itched to hold that doll herself. She had had a rag doll her mother had made for her when she was small, but she had never even seen such a doll as this. It even had lace-edged underclothes!

Helen's hands explored the doll from top to bottom, then she cradled it in her arms. Often enough, Martha had seen Helen break things she took a dislike to, but she was obviously delighted with this beautiful doll.

The teacher reached out and pressed her fingers into Helen's palm.

"D-O-L-L," she said. "Doll."

Martha stared. Surely the woman knew Helen could not hear her.

Helen pushed the teacher's fingers away impatiently, needing both hands free for holding her new doll.

"She loves it," Mrs. Keller told the teacher. "It is beautiful, Miss Annie."

Miss Annie was smiling at the picture the little girl made.

Martha wrapped her arms tightly around herself, holding in all her mixed-up feelings, and left the room quietly. She knew the family would not miss her. And they would not guess how badly she wanted to snatch that doll away from Helen, who'd begun stroking its hair and re-examining its frilly clothes with eager fingers.

As Martha reached the door, Helen's mother let out a big breath. Martha knew just how she felt. She must be hoping Helen might soon stop bursting into wild fits of temper. Could this doll be the first step?

Martha got halfway to the cookhouse before she stopped cold. The *doll* was not what mattered. Helen would soon put it aside — or break it, as she did so many things. Right now Miss Annie was seeing Helen being good, but dinnertime was coming. What would the teacher think when she saw how the family ate?

It was not going to be simple. Miss Annie would surely be shocked at the way Helen left her own dinner to snatch whatever she wanted from the others' plates.

"It's shameful," Sadie Washington had often said, shaking her head. "They let her act as though she's a wild animal."

Martha could only nod.

Now Mrs. Keller had taken Miss Annie and Helen out into the garden, probably to keep Helen calmed down until it was time to eat.

Martha slipped back into the empty room. She longed to touch Helen's doll when nobody was watching. Sure enough, the doll was lying face down in the big easy chair. Careful not to make a sound, Martha took her up and straightened out her tumbled skirts. She found the bonnet that had been tossed aside and, quick as a flash, put it back on the doll's head, carefully tying the ribbons under her chin. The baby doll smiled ever so sweetly up at her.

Then, footsteps. Someone was coming. In an instant, Helen's doll was back in the chair and Martha was out the door. She moved too fast to be caught, and she was smiling as sweetly as the doll.

8

Dinnertime

When Martha reached the cookhouse, Mama gave her a look that said she knew her daughter was late, but that she did not have time to take her to task about it right then.

"Skedaddle in there and pour the water," Sadie Washington said. "And take these biscuits with you. They can go to the sideboard."

Martha put on her good-little-girl face to stifle a smile. She wanted to be in the dining room to find out what happened when Helen misbehaved. She might start out in her own chair, but soon enough she'd be roaming around, reaching her hand into people's plates and helping herself to their food. She'd cram chunks of it into her mouth and get it smeared all over her face and her dress. How many times had Mama had to help Ella try to get the stains out of Helen's clothes after she'd finished a meal? Too many.

Didn't Mrs. Keller realize that Miss Annie would be shocked?

Sure enough, Miss Annie's eyes grew wide when she saw how Helen was allowed to act. As she pawed through their food, the Kellers did nothing to stop her. Even her mother made no move to change her behaviour. It was as though they did not notice Helen's antics any longer.

Martha fetched and carried dishes from the cookhouse to the table, dawdling so she could watch how the teacher would react. Every servant in the household was curious to see what Miss Annie would do. Even though Mama would pretend to be cross with her for gossiping, Martha knew she would want to be told exactly what went on.

The look on Miss Annie's face was plain to see. When Helen stretched out her hand, already greasy from grabbing slices of meat, to help herself to a fistful of Miss Annie's meal, the teacher did not speak. She simply whisked her plate out of reach.

There was a startled silence as the Kellers stared at her. Martha, seeing Helen's face redden as the plate disappeared, put the water pitcher back on the sideboard and sped out of the room. She raced to the cookhouse to tell her mother what had just occurred.

"That Miss Annie, she couldn't believe how Helen acted," she reported. "She was *flabbergasted.*"

"Good," Sadie Washington said. "Maybe she'll talk them into teaching that child some manners. Now stop chattering and lend a hand with these dishes."

The next night, Martha dawdled again, certain there would be more surprises. Sure enough, Miss Annie insisted Helen sit on her chair, and when she was settled, she spread Helen's napkin over her lap. Everyone waited, barely breathing. The teacher, too, waited to see if Helen would jump up. But when she simply sat quietly on her chair, Miss Annie smiled and took a seat beside her.

A minute later, Martha, handing the breadbasket to the mistress, had a hard time keeping her face blank as Helen deliberately threw her napkin under the table.

James Keller laughed, but his father slammed a fist down on the arm of his chair, preparing to roar at him. Miss Annie started to rise to do battle. Then Helen's mother spoke in a cool, firm voice Martha had not heard before.

"You can run along now, Martha," she said, never taking her eyes off her daughter.

"Yes'm," Martha managed to mumble. Keeping her head bent, but listening hard, she left the dining room as slowly as she dared. She was just outside the door when Helen's father said, "I'm afraid, Miss Annie, that our little girl needs time to get used to you being here. Perhaps we have indulged her too much. You will have to go slowly and make allowances . . ."

"No, sir," Miss Annie said clearly. "You are doing her no favours by treating her as though she cannot learn."

Helen left her place to rush to her father. Captain Keller drew her into the circle of his arm and, ignoring the teacher's words, stroked her cheek. "She can just sit over here by me while we all have our dinner. I'll keep her close by and she won't make any trouble," he said, pressing a biscuit into Helen's hand.

Martha waited for Miss Annie's response. Her eyes were cold and her lips were set.

That Miss Annie must see how Helen is smirking, Martha thought. And Mrs. Keller is going to start crying any minute.

Martha fled across the hall and headed for the cookhouse. It felt as though the Kellers and Annie Sullivan were declaring war, and Martha could not bear to watch.

⁙ *9* ⁙

Miss Annie Gets to Work

That night, Martha had trouble sleeping, thinking about what had gone on at the Kellers' dinner table. When she and Mama were alone early the next morning, Martha asked the question that had kept her awake. "Will Miss Annie go away? If Helen keeps being bad . . . will she leave?"

Sadie Washington stood thinking for a moment. Then she shook her head and grinned. "Well, it would take someone with grit to stand up to Captain Keller the way you say she did. And I've heard the Irish are great fighters. Miss Annie sounds like she's Irish to the backbone."

"But the Captain —"

"Never you mind. I bet that Miss Annie is no quitter," Sadie Washington said. "If she can get the mistress roused up to helping her fight for that child, the two of them won't be beaten. You wait and see."

Mama was right. The teacher began using every minute of the day to teach Helen. She didn't just work on the ordinary things. Getting through to a pupil who could not hear what the teacher said or see anything she showed her seemed impossible to Martha, but from the start, Miss Annie never hesitated. Even though Helen often grew angry at being forced to obey her, the teacher kept at it. And Martha was told she was to help.

"You know where everything is and can fetch and carry when Miss Annie needs something. I've told her she can depend on you," the mistress told Martha.

Martha had nodded and tried to look willing but not let her delight show. Helping Miss Annie was so much better than working in the kitchen. Besides, she wanted to see what the teacher would do to help Helen learn.

On the second day, Helen flew into a tantrum. When she kicked Belle and then struck Martha, neither of them was surprised, but Miss Annie, moving like lightning, grasped Helen's wrists and held on. No matter how hard Helen fought to get free, bracing her body and even trying to bite, her teacher did not loosen her grip until Helen finally gave up and started to howl.

"You will *not* hit anyone or kick that poor old dog," Miss Annie said clearly, as though Helen could hear her. And even though Helen could not, she seemed to get the message.

Martha was stunned by what Miss Annie said. Nobody had ever taken her side that way before. Sometimes when Helen hit Martha, Mrs. Keller would come and take Helen into her arms and rock her or somehow comfort her, often reaching into her pocket for the candies she kept there as a treat to settle Helen down. But she never punished Helen or took Martha's part. Martha had always had to put up with Helen's temper until she could get out of range of her fists.

When Martha opened her mouth to tell the teacher that she was used to being struck, Miss Annie spoke before she could get the words out.

"Helen has to learn that such behaviour is wrong," she said. "You know better, and so do I, because we were taught. It is time Helen learned the same lesson."

Then the teacher drew the tear-streaked, shuddering Helen over to a nearby table and sat her down. Helen shoved the table so hard it crashed to the floor.

Miss Annie took her by the shoulders and moved her bodily until she forced her to raise it. But Helen suddenly grabbed hold of it again and, using all her strength, threw it toward the teacher. The edge of the table smashed into Miss Annie's face. As the teacher clasped her hand to her mouth, Martha, horrified, saw blood running through her fingers. And then Miss Annie was holding two teeth in her hand.

"Mama!" Martha yelled, racing down the stairs to get help. As she reached her mother and stammered out what had just happened, she thought, with a sick feeling, that now the teacher would be bound to give up. How could *anyone* put up with somebody hurting them that way?

But Miss Annie did not.

The next morning, as lessons began, Martha winced at the sight of Miss Annie's swollen face. But the teacher managed to smile at her, even though it clearly hurt her to do it.

"It's a good thing Helen can't see her teacher is toothless," she joked, catching hold of Helen and plunking her down in her chair.

Helen began to sniffle, but Miss Annie was having no nonsense. She pulled out a box containing some beads and a cord on which to string them, and put it into Helen's hands. They were many coloured, which would not matter to Helen, but they were different shapes, too — some long, some fat and round, some triangular.

Martha yearned to reach for them, but didn't. Helen did not reach for them at first, either, but soon she could not resist. Miss Annie guided her hand as she showed Helen what to do.

Now Miss Annie was saying the word *beads* and spelling into Helen's hand again. "B-E-A-D-S," she said.

Martha watched, bewildered. Helen could not hear the word or understand what Miss Annie wanted her to do.

"Sit down for a minute and see how I will teach her," Miss Annie said then. Martha hesitated, but then obeyed. She wanted to understand.

Once the beads were safely strung and Helen had had a drink of milk, Miss Annie showed Helen her repeater pocket watch. "Watch, W-A-T-C-H," she said, saying the word as she spelled it with her fingers.

Martha yearned to try making the letter shapes as Miss Annie kept saying the word and spelling it into Helen's hand. Would Helen learn to read this way? If only she, Martha, knew how to read. But the Captain would not allow the servant children to be taught. "A total waste of time," she'd heard him say to James more than once.

Suddenly Martha heard her mother calling. She jumped up and turned to go.

"Don't worry, Martha. You'll be seeing plenty of finger spelling from now on," Miss Annie said quietly from behind her.

Martha stopped and stared over her shoulder. Had the teacher called her by *name*? She *had*. She was not like Miss Temple, who only paid attention to white children.

Martha ran to the cookhouse, eager to tell her mother what the Yankee teacher was up to. Finger spelling! Mama would be amazed.

❊ 10 ❊

The New Plan

Whenever Helen's father happened upon Miss Annie making Helen behave, he would beg her to be gentle with his poor little pet. Martha had to turn her face away to keep her grin from showing. Helen was far too tough to be anybody's pet.

One day Martha was crouched down picking up beads Helen had spilled on the floor in a corner of the schoolroom when Helen's father stopped in yet again and, as Miss Annie made Helen stay sitting down, told the teacher she was being too strict. Martha shrank back out of sight and held her breath.

Her mouth fell open when she heard Miss Annie snap, "Your dogs are better trained than your daughter, Captain Keller," and tell him that Helen was a *person*, not a *pet*.

Martha could not believe her ears. It was absolutely true, of course, but nobody else would have had the nerve to tell him so. He went red as a beet and spluttered something about not putting up with such impertinence.

When Martha reported Miss Annie's words to her mother, Sadie Washington beamed and silently clapped her hands.

Before the teacher started working on getting Helen to tie a bow, she surprised Martha by making *her* do it, too, with her eyes closed. Martha guessed she must have been looking as though anyone in the whole world could tie a bow easily, until Miss Annie proved to her that it was much harder when you couldn't *see*. Day by day, Martha was coming to understand the challenges Helen faced when Miss Annie was trying to teach her: how to eat not with her fingers, but using a spoon and fork; how to dress herself. There was so much for Helen to learn, and maybe the hardest part was that she had no idea *why* she had to master any of the skills.

At least Helen had grown wary of hitting her, Martha thought. Whenever she tried to, Miss Annie would refuse to give her the cake she wanted, or let her make another bead necklace, until she had sat on her chair without stirring for five minutes.

Always, always, always, whatever they were doing,

Miss Annie kept spelling words into Helen's hand. It was clear as day to Martha that this made no sense to Helen and, even though Miss Annie rewarded her for keeping at it, Helen seemed to find the whole process infuriating.

There were also constant interruptions from Helen's father and mother, from Ella and Viney, and once in a while from James, who enjoyed being difficult and teasing the teacher.

Martha felt sorry for Miss Annie — although she did not say so, even to her mother.

But she could not grasp why Helen's learning to spell mattered so much.

❧ *11* ❧

Helen's Revenge

One day, Helen managed to grab the key to the teacher's bedroom door. When Miss Annie was in the room, Helen turned the key and shut her in. Then she ran and hid the key where nobody would find it.

When Miss Annie called to be let out, Martha was the first to guess what Helen had done. It was just like that afternoon she had locked her mother in the pantry. Fearing it would do no good, still Martha tried to make Helen show where she had hidden the key. But Helen just laughed and darted out into the garden.

When Martha chased after her and caught her, Helen put her hands behind her back and laughed harder. Martha was tempted to shake Helen, but knew she couldn't. The minute Martha let her go, Helen ran back into the house and tore up and down the hall. Even when her mother wept and searched her for the key, Helen would not give in.

Everyone sought high and low, but no key came to light.

Martha winced as Helen's father bellowed at all of them that they should have kept a stricter eye on his daughter. His wife shrank against the wall as he roared threats at all and sundry.

In the end, Captain Keller had to climb a ladder and carry Miss Annie out through the window and down to the ground. The teacher protested, but Helen's father, red in the face from effort and outrage, insisted he do it his way. The family and the servants all gathered around the ladder to watch, and although he shouted at them to leave they went only a little way off, then ventured back. It was far too good a show to miss.

Martha, standing near the mistress, heard her mutter, "Oh, please, don't let Miss Annie leave over this."

But by now Martha was sure Miss Annie would do no such thing. She remembered the day when Helen had tried to pull her hand away, sick of constantly having words spelled into her palm, and the teacher had said, "No you don't, young lady. I will *not* let you give up. I will help you find the key."

When Martha had stared at Miss Annie, knowing she must realize Helen could not understand a word she said, the teacher had looked right back at her.

"Martha, sit down and listen to me," she commanded. "This is the most important thing I can teach Helen. If I can get her to know words, she will be able to think and read and talk to you."

She told Martha to close her eyes and cover her ears and then try to think without words.

Martha obeyed, even though she felt silly. But when she tried to think without words, they kept coming into her mind however hard she struggled to keep them out. She opened her eyes and gazed at Helen's teacher.

Miss Annie was grinning. "Well, how was it?" she asked.

"I couldn't do it," Martha mumbled.

"No," Miss Annie said. "And Helen can't think properly without language, either. She doesn't even know what it means to think the way you and I do. But, Martha, once she gets to realize words exist, the world will open to her.

"We won't ever be able to give her eyesight or hearing," the teacher went on quietly. "But we can give her so much. That is why I have to stick at it, however long it takes. Some day she will understand."

Miss Annie kept on and on with the finger spelling,

even though Helen tried to pull her hand away whenever she was forced to work at it. But no matter how much Helen sulked or protested, Miss Annie constantly spelled words into her hand, using the manual alphabet designed for the deafblind, and made Helen spell them back. When Helen did, Miss Annie gave her a bite of cake or her doll to hold and told her she was a "good girl."

✤ *12* ✤

Martha Lends a Hand

Martha was out in the garden, weeding, when she heard Miss Annie calling her. Happy to have an excuse to stop, she dropped the trowel and ran to see what the teacher wanted.

She found Miss Annie in the room where she worked with Helen. Scarlet in the face, Helen was

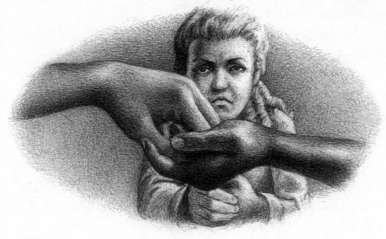

backed up to the wall, her hands clenched into fists. Martha knew that stony look on Helen's face. She was going to fight anyone who came within reach, even if the someone was Miss Annie. Martha's heart sank.

The teacher was moving a chair over close to Helen. She set it down with a *thump* Helen would be sure to feel. Then she seated herself in it, landing heavily. Her cheeks were as red as Helen's, and her eyes showed that she was as set on getting her way as Helen was.

"Martha, come here and hold out your hand," she commanded.

Martha hesitated. Then she murmured, "She won't give in, Miss."

"Come," Miss Annie repeated.

Head down, Martha obeyed.

Without explaining what was happening, Miss Annie took Martha's hand and began to spell words into it. "M-A-R-T-H-A, Martha," Miss Annie said loudly, spelling each letter into Martha's trembling palm. "I'll do it once more, and then you see if you can spell it back."

Martha felt torn. Part of her wanted to run away from the two of them, and another part filled with excitement as she did her best to make the letters with her fingers.

M-A-R-T-H-A. She could hardly believe she was spelling her own name.

Now Miss Annie was waving her arms, stirring up the air so Helen could not help knowing they were doing something. She shifted the chair, too, and dropped a heavy book onto the floor, grinning as she saw Helen jump.

Miss Annie reached for Martha's hand and finger spelled her name again, smiling as Martha copied the actions perfectly this time.

It took a few minutes for Helen to realize that they were busy and she was being shut out. She stood stiffly, straining to guess where they were and who had been brought in to play a part. When she at last realized what was happening, she stamped over to the chair where Miss Annie sat with Martha pulled up next to her. She thrust Martha aside so roughly that she nearly crashed headlong onto the floor. Although Helen could not speak, her message was crystal clear. Miss Annie was *hers*! And *her* Miss Annie had nothing whatsoever to do with Martha Washington.

When Miss Annie reached for Helen's hand, though, and Helen jerked away again, Miss Annie pulled Martha back beside her to go on with the lesson.

"She's getting mad, Miss Annie. She'll hit us,"

Martha cried out, preparing to duck.

"No, I won't let her. She'll come around," the teacher declared. "Wait and see. She won't be able to help herself. All bright children are full of curiosity, Martha, and this child is bright."

Sure enough, Helen, still red in the face and breathing heavily, pushed in again. This time she stuck out her hand.

"Martha, move away a little," Miss Annie said in a low voice. "But wait there."

Martha stood still. Her stomach knotted as she tried to understand what the teacher wanted from her.

When Helen allowed the lesson to begin, Miss Annie whispered that Martha could leave now.

Martha crept out the door and then sped straight to the kitchen to tell her mother what had just happened.

Ella was there, taking a break from ironing. She had been Helen's nanny when she was little, and she'd been kicked and pinched as much as Martha and Belle. As Martha poured out her story, Ella shook her head. "I say that child's possessed. She's got a devil inside her and that's a fact."

Mama shot a sharp look at Ella. "Don't talk such nonsense, woman," she snapped. "Helen's no more *possessed* than you are. Think back to the bright baby we knew before she was sick. If they leave that Miss Annie be, she'll do the poor mite a powerful lot of good."

"I do remember. Helen was a ray of sunshine back then," Ella said softly.

Martha smiled and ran back to the room where Miss Annie was working with Helen. She had not told even her mother that she'd made up her mind to learn whatever Helen was being taught.

In the days that followed, Martha took every chance she got to copy what Helen was being shown. Miss Annie caught her finger spelling and smiled. "Excellent," she said. Martha sighed with relief. She had been afraid she would be in trouble if they found out what she was up to. She knew what Captain Keller thought about sending any of the servant children to school. Her own mother had heard him say that book learning would just go to their heads and get them into trouble, and he wasn't putting up with it. He didn't seem to believe that Martha or any of the others on his land should learn their letters.

But Mama was pleased when Martha confided that Miss Annie was teaching her. "You mind what she tells you, daughter," she said.

Martha nodded. Clearly Mama did not want her to grow up ignorant, whatever Helen's father said.

❧ *13* ❧

Martha Helps

In bed at night, Martha began stringing words together. She was grateful that Miss Annie almost always said the words aloud as she spelled them into Helen's palm, one by one. Martha did it in the dark, but so did Helen, so it seemed right. It wasn't like regular printing words on paper, she knew, but it was going to give Helen words she understood and could actually read. Miss Annie told her about blind people reading Braille. It was hard to believe this, but Martha knew Miss Annie would not lie. If it happened, and it would, it would be a miracle.

She was sitting on the porch, waiting for the Captain to bring Helen back from a walk through the far stretch of the garden, when Percy came up behind her. Swiftly she clasped her hands together in her lap, but not before he saw her practising finger spelling.

"What're you doing, Martha?" he demanded,

dropping into a squat in the patch of shade next to where she sat.

"Nothing," she said, pulling a grass stem and chewing the sweet tip.

"I think you're copying what Miss Annie's always doing," he said. "Is Helen learning something from doing those things?"

Seeing the Captain approaching with Helen, Martha stood up. "Never you mind what I do, Percy," she said under her breath. Then, louder, "You'd better move along before the Captain sees you."

She turned back to look at him and discovered he had already gone. If Captain Keller caught Percy not working at something, he'd be in trouble, but Percy was so quick that he hardly ever did get caught.

She certainly would not want Helen's father to catch *her* finger spelling, either.

Did he understand that if Helen kept on learning, his precious daughter might be able to read someday? At times Martha herself had trouble believing that either she or Helen would really be able to learn how. She was not even sure why she longed so to be able to do it. Mama couldn't read well. She knew lots of stories and she knew all her recipes by heart, but she never looked for a book. Only the white folks did it without thinking. But Martha felt sure that it would somehow change her if she could learn. Besides, Mama was always pleased when she saw Martha learning anything new. Martha had not dreamed of being able to read until the teacher had come to work with Helen. Now maybe . . . just maybe . . . she might someday manage to do it.

That same day, Miss Annie came up behind Martha when she was sitting in the corner practising the letters she had memorized.

"Have you got the whole alphabet off by heart now?" she asked.

Martha stared up at her, not knowing what to say.

"I could teach you words if you like, Martha," she said, speaking softly. "When Helen is busy with her mother, or napping." It took Martha a stunned minute to believe what Miss Annie had said. Then she nodded her head so hard that her curls bounced.

Miss Annie smiled at her. "I want you to learn not only for your own sake, but for Helen's," she explained. "When Helen can speak by finger spelling, she'll need people to talk to. I will be one, of course, and her mother is learning in the evenings — but Helen will want to talk to other people, too. She will long to speak with another girl sometimes."

Martha had guessed that the mistress was learning to make the letters, because she had seen her busily spelling hidden letters in her lap when she was supposed to be reading or mending.

Martha knew why Mrs. Keller practised her finger spelling secretly and never spoke openly about her progress. The Captain was still unhappy with the way Miss Annie made his little girl obey her. He wanted Helen to learn, but hated to see her being forced to do anything that he believed made her unhappy.

He never lowered his voice when he was telling his wife how he felt, so the whole household knew.

"She asks too much of the child," he would insist, striding back and forth as he let loose his complaints. "Surely you can't really believe Helen will ever be able to communicate with others like a normal child. That young woman is forcing her to know she *can't* be like the rest of us. Rubbing salt in the wound — that's what she's doing. It is cruel."

More and more often, he would interfere with Helen's lessons. He ignored Miss Annie as he swept in and took his daughter away. Miss Annie put up with it at first, hoping he would realize Helen needed to concentrate until she completed a task. She tried to explain but he brushed her words and explanations aside, insisting that he was Helen's father and he knew best what she needed.

Helen's half-brother followed his father's example. Helen soon discovered that if she could escape from her teacher and run to her father or to James, they would take her away for a carriage ride or a walk in the garden.

"The Missus is going to have to make them leave her be," Martha's mother declared when she saw what was happening.

Martha knew Mrs. Keller was on Miss Annie's side, but she could not imagine her speaking up strongly enough to make the Captain stop interfering.

Still, she *did* stand up to him when Helen misbehaved at dinner, now. Martha had only seen it happen a couple of times, though. Maybe the mistress would grow brave enough to keep trying, for Helen's sake.

Finally Miss Annie demanded to be given time alone with Helen, telling the Kellers that unless she was allowed to take complete charge of her and permitted to do as she thought best, Helen would remain more animal than human. She had not actually threatened to leave, but Martha knew Helen's mother must be worried sick that the teacher would decide to give up.

Maybe that was what gave her the courage to insist to the Captain that Miss Annie have her way. At last they all agreed to try the plan the teacher had outlined.

Right away, Martha was caught up in the preparations. "Today is moving day, Martha. Pray for me," Miss Annie murmured as they met on the porch of the Little House. "And I'll need your help. You can bring things over when Helen is asleep and leave them outside the door for me to find."

The first step was to rearrange the furniture there, making the rooms so different that Helen would not recognize the place. Martha was kept busy helping to shift footstools and end tables. She worked hard and hoped against hope it would "do the trick," as her mother said, and make Helen believe she was someplace away from her parents entirely.

Once the place was so changed Helen would have no idea where she was, Miss Annie took her out in the carriage and drove for miles. Since Helen could not see the countryside they passed, she was soon lost.

Percy carried buckets of water and left them outside the door for the teacher to use, and Martha delivered trays of food. She also filled a small basket with nuts and other treats, covering them tightly so Belle would not nose into the basket, and placed it next to the water. When it was gone the next morning, she felt like dancing.

Martha also stole to the window and peeped in when it was safe. Miss Annie saw her but they made no signals to each other in case they might alert Helen. At first, Helen seemed to be crying or throwing things or striking Miss Annie. Martha felt heartbroken watching them battle. But a couple of days later, she saw Helen leaning against her teacher. Both of them looked worn out, but they must have made peace.

Then Helen really began to learn. Her mother and sometimes even the Captain would watch through the window, the way Martha had done. Martha heard them telling each other that Helen would be coming home to them in no time. She knew they were wrong. Helen made a step forward but, a day later, fought against Miss Annie as though she hated her. Her parents had not seen her backsliding, but Martha wished they would.

Helen's parents grew more and more thrilled with the changes.

They saw Helen sitting on a chair, working on a wooden puzzle and feeding herself using a spoon and fork without spilling. A day or two later, they watched her dress herself and spell words into her teacher's hand without fussing. Finally the Kellers sent Martha with a note to say they wished to speak to the teacher the next afternoon when Helen was napping.

Miss Annie picked up the slip of paper Martha had slid under the door and came out, leaving Helen busy dressing a doll.

"I thought they would be wanting to cut our time short," she said. "They see her progress — I've noticed them watching — and they want Helen back home. But she's *not* ready. Oh, Martha, I do hope I can persuade them not to take her back yet."

Martha wanted to say she thought they might agree to stick to Miss Annie's plans, but she, too, was afraid they would not.

She followed behind when the Kellers set out. When Miss Annie slipped out the door of the Little House, they praised everything she had accomplished with their daughter.

"You've worked wonders with her," Mrs. Keller gushed. "She's like a normal child. We're so grateful."

"Yes. Wonderful," Helen's father barked, staring at the ground.

The teacher listened as they went on and on, but she looked tired. Finally she tried to tell them how much it mattered that she keep Helen with her longer.

"We think she should come home *now*. Oh, she's changed so much it is unbelievable," the mistress kept on. "We're convinced she's ready to come home."

"We have a *long* way to go yet," Annie Sullivan insisted.

"Yes. But I miss her so," Helen's mother pleaded. "We want her to come home. I promise we will keep up your good work. We will be firm with her."

"Obedience is not enough, Mrs. Keller," Miss Annie said. "Helen has made a beginning, but there is so much more she must learn. I *beg* you to leave her with me."

"Enough. We will have her back tomorrow," the

Captain snapped, turning to march away, pulling his wife along behind him. The next day, they came to collect her.

When Helen found herself back in her mother's arms, she pranced like a pony that had just been set free in the meadow. She was whooping, too, and although the wordless sounds were wild, they were clearly filled with glee. Martha felt a lump in her throat. Their joy in being reunited was lovely to see.

Martha knew Mama would be expecting her to follow the family home, but she hesitated. Miss Annie was still gazing after them.

She looks lonely, Martha thought. The idea startled her. Unsure what she ought to do, she moved closer to the teacher and waited.

Miss Annie gave her a crooked smile. "Well, Martha," she said, "that's that. We did our best."

Martha swallowed and asked the question she longed to have answered. "Does she know the meaning of words yet?"

Miss Annie remained silent for what seemed a long time. Then she shook her head. "Not yet," she said through clenched teeth. "But she will. She will."

"She's much better in other ways," Martha ventured. "They're so happy."

"She will test that happiness before the day is over," Miss Annie said grimly. "Oh, Martha, they don't know what they're in for."

Martha did not understand until evening. Helen had behaved beautifully all that day, but at the dinner table she began misbehaving as she had when Miss Annie first arrived. She slid off her chair, dropping her napkin onto the floor and knocking her glass over so the water splashed across the tablecloth.

Miss Annie sprang up, but before she could force Helen to return to her chair, Captain Keller gathered his daughter into his arms and fended the teacher off. "She won't do it again," he said. "I'll keep her here."

Miss Annie faced him head-on. "I thought you wanted her to learn to behave like a normal child," she said.

Martha, coming in the doorway, thought sparks were shooting out of the teacher's eyes. She looked over at the Captain, dreading the argument she was certain was coming.

But Helen's mother stunned them all by rising to her feet and saying in a voice that shook, but was determined, "Let go of Helen, Captain. Miss Annie is right. You must see that now. We promised we would do as she says."

Martha blinked. She got ready for one of the Captain's outbursts, but it didn't come. When it didn't, even though Martha had to go back to the cookhouse, she knew Helen was going to end up back on her chair. As Mama had said at the start, if the mistress and Miss Annie joined forces, the two of them would win. "Miss Annie is tough," Mama had said, "and the mistress's love for Helen will make her strong, too."

As usual, Mama was right — even though there were plenty more battles to get through in the following days.

When Martha told Mama about the standoff, her mother said, "You wait. The Captain likes Helen being more polite at the table."

"But he doesn't seem to care about her learning words," Martha muttered.

"Hmm, I suppose he wants her to be good, not clever," Sadie Washington said thoughtfully. "But he'll learn, when Helen does."

Martha wondered about that. *Would* Helen ever really break through to understanding what words were *for*? She glibly spelled back words Miss Annie told her. Martha told herself over and over that surely the miracle must soon happen, but she knew the most important part was still missing. Helen still had no notion of what the letters *meant*. She was like a parrot. She seemed to spell back words, but really she was just mimicking her teacher, not realizing that what she spelled was filled with meaning.

It was a game to her, one she was good at, but still just a game.

When she wanted cake, she would finger spell the word, but it was a trick she performed — motions of her hands that would bring her what she wanted, like her old sign of spectacles to mean her father, or cutting a slice of bread to ask for some.

Until Martha herself began to be able to talk to Helen's teacher by finger spelling, and understand the teacher's answers to her, she did not completely know the difference between how she could use words and Helen could not. Once, after watching Miss Annie spelling a word for Helen and catching the blank look on Helen's face, Martha's eyes stung with sudden tears. It was so *unfair*. And it was not right. It was as though she and Helen had been given presents, and when they opened them, Martha's held something wonderful, but Helen's box was empty.

"Once Helen grasps the first word, it will be clear sailing," the teacher told Martha and Helen's mother again and again. "If we just keep at it, one day, I promise you, she will find the key. Wait and see."

But day after day passed without it happening.

And however hard Martha struggled to hold on to Miss Annie's promise, she felt herself starting to lose hope.

When she became truly downhearted, she took to scrambling up the tree from which she had rescued Helen, and perching there, calmed by the leaves rustling around her and murmuring comfort. But even though it helped a little, she was still discouraged.

✣ *14* ✣

Hand in Hand

One morning, Miss Annie had such a bad headache that she had to lie down in her darkened bedroom. At first, Helen's mother sat next to her, bathing her forehead with cool water, but finally the teacher told her she just needed to be left alone until it was over.

Mrs. Keller brought Helen out to the cookhouse where Martha, with tears pouring down her cheeks, was peeling and chopping onions to go into the pickles Mama was making.

Seeing her, the mistress laughed. Then she said, "I'm sorry, Sadie, but I need Martha to take Helen outside and keep her playing quietly while Miss Annie gets over her headache."

Martha grinned and promptly put down her paring knife. Mama sighed and picked it up.

"Run along," she said. "And do keep the noise

down. That poor Miss Annie really suffers with those headaches."

Martha took Helen out to the front garden, far away from Miss Annie's room, pausing on the way to pick up two of Helen's dolls. Glancing at the house as they passed, she saw Mrs. Keller at her desk, writing letters. She looked up as they went by and smiled. Martha smiled back and led Helen across the grass to sit on the bank next to the drive. Soon they were happily changing the dolls' dresses. Then she heard a horse, pulling a delivery wagon, turning off the road. Wondering who it could be, she glanced up just in time to see the animal shy at something and plunge sideways. The startled driver gave a bellow, which sent the animal into a total panic. Horse and wagon came thundering down the long drive.

It took Martha a moment to realize that they might be in danger. Then she jumped up and reached for Helen. Even though Helen could not see the oncoming horse or hear the pounding noise its hoofs made, she could feel the ground start to shake beneath her. She scrambled to her feet faster than Martha, but instead of running to where it was safe, she began to dash directly *into* the path of the runaway horse.

Martha screamed and dove after her.

She was almost too late, but she just managed to snatch at Helen's flailing right hand and yank her backward up the bank. The two of them toppled over onto the grass and lay with their hands clasped, holding tight to each other as the horse went hurtling by. The delivery man, still fighting desperately to get control of it, was yelling cuss words at the top of his voice, but Martha hardly heard him. Her heart was pounding, and she was gasping for breath and clinging to Helen's hand.

When the horse and wagon had careened past and swerved around the house toward the stable, Martha realized that although Helen was clearly shaken, she was laughing. What's more, her hand, in Martha's, felt unlike it had ever felt before.

Martha had often held that hand as she pulled Helen after her to the stable, or up the stairs, or out to the cookhouse. Always Helen had fought to get free, struggling to loosen Martha's grip and escape.

But now, she clung to Martha's fingers as though they comforted her.

At this moment, Martha was not in charge of taking Helen somewhere, and Helen was not fighting to get free.

It's as though I'm her friend, Martha thought.

She remembered telling her mother that she and Helen could never really be friends, not when Helen could not see or hear her. It was not possible, she had said.

But I was wrong, she thought. Maybe we're friends right now.

There was still a great space between them, of course. They could not speak to each other of their feelings. And they lived in different worlds.

But this minute, they were hand in hand, and somehow equal in a way they had never been before.

"Hand-in-hand friends," Martha murmured. Still holding on, Helen sat up and smiled.

Then Mrs. Keller came running from the house and swept her child into her arms and bore her away, taking her back into her life as daughter of the house.

Yet, as Martha got up and started to go to tell her mother about their close call, she was still holding on to how she had felt when she and Helen were hand in hand for those few seconds. She did not find words for what had happened, but somehow she knew something between them had changed, something deep inside both of them. Whatever it was, it linked her to Helen in a way neither of them had been before. And, even though the memory of it was fading away already, as she crossed the garden, Martha knew that holding Helen's hand that way had mattered.

Nearing the house and peering through the front window, she glimpsed the mistress feeding Helen something. A gingersnap probably. Helen loved those. If she went to the cookhouse, would Mama have a treat waiting for her? Or only more onions to peel?

Laughing, Martha turned and started back to get the dolls, which they had left on the bank. If she hadn't remembered, they would have been rained on for sure. And both Helen's mother and hers would have scolded her about it.

Martha tucked Nancy under her arm and cradled Rosabelle close. Then she dawdled, giving Mama time to finish making her pickles.

Wondering if her mother had heard about the horse almost running Helen down, she walked a little faster. If Mama had been told, Martha knew she would get an extra hug. No gingersnaps, but she wouldn't trade mothers with Helen.

Then she saw Mama coming to look for her and she began to run.

✣ 15 ✣

The Day the World Changed

The next morning, baby Mildred was teething and had started to howl. Nothing Ella did could calm her, and the mistress was out. When the doorbell rang, Ella handed the howling baby to Martha while she went to see who was there.

"Hush, hush, little Miss Mildred," Martha crooned, gently joggling the baby up and down and making her name into a song.

After a moment, Mildred broke off wailing and stared up at Martha. Then she put her thumb in her mouth and closed her eyes.

Martha lifted the baby until the top of her downy head was tucked under her chin. She could feel Mildred breathing softly in and out against her throat.

It was like that bit in the Bible, the part that said, "my cup runneth over."

By the time Ella came back, the baby was so sound

asleep that nothing short of a tornado would have wakened her.

"You sure have a way with her, Martha," Ella said softly, taking the baby to the cradle for her nap.

Martha hardly ever had a chance to rock Mildred that way. What with Aunt Evelyn, the mistress, Viney and Ella, there was always a grown woman waiting to care for her. So Martha was smiling as she left.

She was still feeling pleased with herself when Mama sent her up with the milk and cookies Miss Annie and Helen always had for their morning break.

The minute she reached the schoolroom door, however, Martha knew things were not going well. Helen was huffing and stamping her feet.

Clutching the tray, Martha hesitated, unsure whether she should go in or come back later.

Helen flew into rages much less often these days, but now and then she and Miss Annie locked horns over something, and Helen remembered exactly how to stage a tantrum. Martha peeked in just as Helen knocked over the chair next to her and hurled her body backwards against the bookcase.

"Come on in, Martha," Miss Annie called, ignoring Helen.

Even though she knew she need not be quiet,

Martha tiptoed across the floor and put the tray down on the table next to where the teacher was sitting. She had two of Helen's dolls on her lap — Nancy and Rosabelle, the ones they had played with the day before. Martha eyed them, trying not to let her surprise show.

Miss Annie chuckled.

"I'm trying to teach her that the word *doll* means *all* dolls, not just one," she explained. "Have a cookie first, Martha, and then I think you can help me."

Helen was still up against the bookcase, her face flushed, her fists clenched and her feet kicking at the chair she had toppled over.

When Martha had gobbled down one of the cookies, Miss Annie smiled and beckoned. "Come over here," she said. "Let's see if we can get her to calm down first."

Martha thought of how easy it had been to quiet Helen's baby sister. Rocking her and singing softly had done the trick. But Helen would not hear a song and was far too big to rock.

Miss Annie picked up the chair and stood it on its legs with a *bang* Helen would feel. Then she motioned to Martha to sit down on it.

Then the teacher went over to Helen, took hold

of her arm and firmly drew her, struggling, back to where they had been sitting. Gripping Helen's elbow too tightly for her to wrench away, the teacher picked up Rosabelle in her free hand and tried to force Helen to take her.

Martha looked away, unable to bear watching the two of them handling Rosabelle so roughly.

She was certain the doll felt hurt by their sharp fingers gripping her, yet there was no way she could make them stop. She clenched her teeth and blinked back tears. How could they treat the lovely doll that way?

"Be careful," she whispered. "Don't drop her."

If only Rosabelle had been given to her instead of Helen, the doll would have been held as gently as Mildred had been earlier.

But Rosabelle didn't simply slip out of their hands. Instead, Helen grabbed hold of the beautiful porcelain doll, wrenched her away from Miss Annie and flung her onto the floor as hard as she could.

"No, Helen!" Martha cried. But, even if Helen could have heard her, it was too late. Rosabelle lay shattered into dozens of fragments around their feet.

Helen began shrieking with laughter while she trampled the broken bits, filled with triumph at her show of power.

Martha had loved that doll from the moment Helen had lifted her out of Miss Annie's valise. Even though she knew no doll like it would ever belong to her, she had often pretended she owned Rosabelle. Sometimes she had planned to steal her away and hide her where Helen would never find her.

Closing her eyes so she would not have to see Rosabelle's smashed body, Martha had all she could do not to pull back her arm and give Helen's face a stinging slap. The temptation was so strong that she raced out of the room and went pelting out to the cookhouse. There she could pour out to her mother the tragic story. She had never told her mother how she felt about Helen's doll, but Mama would know.

Sadie Washington gently stroked Martha's wet cheeks as she listened to the story. Then she picked up the bucket by the back door and handed it to her daughter. Keeping busy was the best way she knew to deal with sorrow.

"Martha, crying won't mend matters. You go and fetch me in a pail of water. Then we can make some dessert for their supper," she said. "You choose which one and we'll make enough for us to have some, too."

If she had stayed in the schoolroom, Martha would have heard Miss Annie counting to ten and then, ignoring Helen, sweeping up the bits of porcelain. The teacher made herself stop dwelling on Martha's grief-stricken face. Helen clearly had no idea that she had hurt Martha when she'd destroyed the doll. Glancing at her, Miss Annie saw she was still pleased with herself. She had not understood that now her doll was gone forever.

When she was done sweeping up the bits, Helen's teacher took her by the hand and led her out into the garden.

The minute Helen understood where they were headed, she began to skip. She loved going out where there were not so many rules. She loved drinking in the fragrant scents of the roses, which her father prized, and feeling the wind ruffle her curls. The spreading garden was the playground where she and Martha spent happy hours together. Now she and Miss Annie went down the path side by side. The teacher, never ceasing to teach, stopped to spell out everything they passed. Even though Helen was bored with the word game, she imitated Miss Annie automatically, although her real attention was given to enjoying the sweet scents that spoke of spring.

Martha was at the wellhouse ahead of them. She had begun filling the bucket when she saw them start down the path. She ducked her head so she would not have to face them. She did not want even Miss Annie to see the tearstains on her cheeks.

Annie Sullivan had stopped walking to watch her, but Martha did not lift her head.

The teacher sighed and spoke. "Martha, just a moment. Will you please pump some water over Helen's hand while I hold it out?" she said.

Martha wanted to refuse. But she couldn't. Miss Annie had taught her the alphabet and had started her learning to spell words. Not only that, but she treated her differently from anyone else. Mama loved her, she knew, and the others, especially Percy and Minta, liked her. But Miss Annie made Martha feel like someone who mattered.

Then, all at once, she remembered how she had felt yesterday, lying on the grass hand in hand with Helen. They had been friends.

Without speaking, she put down the partially filled bucket and lifted the pump handle.

The teacher held out Helen's open hand so the water would flow over it. At the same time she wrote the letters W-A-T-E-R into Helen's other palm.

Martha watched as Miss Annie spelled the word first slowly, and then did it again more quickly.

Suddenly Helen grew rigid and began to tremble. Martha and Miss Annie both stared at her. What had made her stiffen that way? Her face was twisting strangely, too, and she was making a sound Martha had not heard before. Yet it was vaguely familiar.

Then Martha was jolted by a memory of a long-ago day. She had been four or five and Helen had not yet lost her sight and hearing. Martha remembered the toddler looking up at her and holding out her empty cup to be filled. "Wawa," she had said.

"Water," Martha whispered. Was that the sound?

Hearing her, Miss Annie went as rigid as Helen. She went on finger spelling the word while she, too, watched Helen's lips moving. Could she possibly be trying to say the one word everyone had heard her repeat before the sickness had robbed her of not only her hearing and sight, but her speech? Could this be the moment they had been waiting for?

Annie Sullivan and Martha, standing side by side, were both caught up by Helen's desperate struggle to speak the one word she had remembered as water gushed across her upturned palm.

Martha tugged at the teacher's skirt and gave a jump for joy. But before she could shout out what she had guessed, Annie Sullivan whispered, "Wait."

Martha was confused, but she closed her lips and made herself hush. Was the teacher afraid they would somehow startle Helen?

Martha stared up at Miss Annie. She was holding her breath and tears had begun to slide out from under her dark glasses and spill down her cheeks.

If *water* was the first word, the one that would turn out to be the key to unlock Helen's prison door, the two of them must take care Helen did not lose it.

Then Helen put out her one hand, and with the other, thumped herself on the chest. Martha stared at her, trying to guess what she meant, but her teacher understood at once.

With shaking fingers, she spelled Helen's name into her outstretched hand.

Martha had long since stopped pumping.

Gazing at the other two, she struggled to grasp exactly what was going on. The two of them were finger spelling, of course, but something new was happening.

Helen's face had grown radiant. Martha watched as she struck her palm against Miss Annie next, demanding her second word.

This time, the woman spelled T-E-A-C-H-E-R.

Helen flung her arms around Miss Annie's waist

and hugged her with all her might. Then she pulled her along as she swung around and hurried toward the house. Martha could see Mrs. Keller standing on the porch, trying to make sense out of what she was seeing.

From her place by the wellhouse, Martha watched the mistress staring at the two racing toward her. Then Helen cannoned into her mother. She patted her and stretched out that eager hand to her teacher once again.

"M-O-T-H-E-R," Annie spelled. "Mother."

As her fingers gave the word to Helen, she said it aloud in an unsteady voice so Helen's mother could hear.

Martha, waiting stock-still by the pump, suddenly recalled Miss Annie telling them what would happen when Helen understood what one word meant. Now it had happened, and Martha had been there.

Now Mrs. Keller had taken in the miracle, and gathered her daughter into her arms. Helen clasped her closely in return, but then pulled free, unable to stay still. Twirling in a joyous circle, she brushed against Belle, who was standing close beside her.

Out went her hand, impatient for another word.

Gazing at the little group on the porch, Martha was

filled with longing. If only she could run and join them. But she was suddenly shy. She was not a Keller, after all. She was only the cook's daughter. They might not want her.

"Martha, come here where Helen can reach you!" Annie Sullivan called.

And Sadie Washington's daughter, with a whoop of delight, ran to have her name spelled into her friend's waiting hand.

Author's Note

Helen Keller lost her vision and hearing when she was one-and-a-half and did not learn what words were until she was almost seven. During those years, children learn so much that it is astonishing. You learn to crawl, walk, run, skip and hop, climb up and down. Helen learned to do these things, but she could not learn to watch out for obstacles. She fell often and hurt herself.

You also learn language. You need to know such simple words as "No" and "Watch out" and "Come here" and "I love you." Helen never heard these words spoken.

You learn to count and to sing and to call people and to answer questions. You learn people's names and which one is your mother and who are strangers. Helen could not learn any of this. You learn to talk and to listen. And, most important of all, perhaps, you learn to use the words you are coming to understand, to *think*. You tell yourself, "I am hungry," and, "I don't want to go," and you begin to ask questions. Helen Keller spent years as a little girl without words, and without even knowing what words were.

I had read lots of books about Helen, all of which told how she did learn language. But none of them dwelt upon the years before Miss Annie came. One day, I began to wonder what her life was like during those early years. I thought I might write a picture book about this. But when I tried, I found that, even though I knew lots of things Helen did, I did not know how she *felt* or *thought*. I needed help.

That was when I discovered Martha.

People keep asking me if this story is true or made up. It is not an easy question to answer. All the people in the book except for Miss Temple and Percy's little sister are based on real people. Almost all the things Helen Keller does here, she actually did. She cut off Martha's hair, locked her mother in the pantry and, later, locked her teacher in her bedroom and refused to show them where the key was hidden. She stole the cake from the kitchen and deliberately broke her porcelain doll. She did crash into things and have tantrums daily before her teacher came. She did throw a table at Miss Annie when the teacher had been with them only a short time, knocking out two of Annie Sullivan's front teeth. These incidents are not made up by me, but written down by Helen herself.

But she did not say how she felt or what she thought. I needed help. I needed Martha.

In her autobiography, *The Story of My Life*, written when she was twenty-one, Helen says that Martha Washington was her constant companion in those early years. She says she could make Martha do whatever she wanted and she tells stories about their escapades.

But she never wondered what life was like for Martha. I wondered, and this book tells what I came to believe.

Helen Keller did not tell us what happened to the cook's daughter once she herself learned words and could use language, not only to communicate, but to think and read and discover the world. With her teacher's help, Helen became a college graduate and travelled widely; she left her shut-in childhood behind. Martha's place in her life was taken over by her teacher, her family and a host of friends.

I wish I knew what happened to Martha later on, but I do know that she was Helen's first friend, and that this friendship mattered enough for Helen to tell about it when she wrote her life story. Like many others who have written about Helen Keller, I found her fascinating. But as I wrote about the two little girls, I grew to love Martha and to believe that she played an enormously important part in Helen's early life, helping her to reach out and care for someone beyond herself.

There were many other people in Helen's world, but most of them were adults who pitied her and looked after her. Martha, "the child of our cook . . . [who] had as great a love of mischief as I," was almost the only child Helen named in her autobiography, the only person she actually played with, the only one who saw past her disabilities to the child she really was. When Miss Annie arrived, she found Helen to be lively and challenging and aware in a way she might not have been if she had not had her "close companion," Martha. Writing the story with an eye to Martha's point of view, I came to believe in and love Martha Washington. Without her help, this book would never have been written.